For Bea & Mila

Copyright © 2020 by Lisa Swerling and Ralph Lazar.

Library of Congress Cataloging-in-Publication Data available.

ISBN 978-1-4521-7982-7

Manufactured in China.

MIX
Paper from
responsible sources
FSC™ C008047

Design by Abbie Goveia.
Typeset in Zemke Hand.

10 9 8 7 6 5 4 3 2

Chronicle Books LLC
680 Second Street
San Francisco, California 94107

Chronicle Books—we see things differently.
Become part of our community at www.chroniclekids.com.

THE SKY IS THE LIMIT

A Celebration of All the Things You Can Do

Lisa Swerling & Ralph Lazar

chronicle books · san francisco

A world full of wonder
is waiting for you . . .

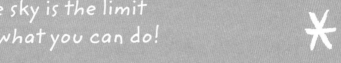

The sky is the limit
of what you can do!

There are roads to be traveled

and dreams to unfold,

magic to conjure

and tales to be told.

Cakes to be gobbled

and spoons to be licked,

cupboards to hide in

and friends to be tricked.

Feet to be tickled
and backs to be scratched . . .

maps to be followed
and plans to be hatched.

Bikes to be ridden

and fences to mend,

fortunes to squirrel

and fortunes to spend.

Trees to be clambered
and bubbles to pop,

lakes to be dived in
and bellies to flop.

Costumes to dazzle

and parties to throw,

and flowers to grow.

Teams to be part of

and trophies to shine,

beans to be planted

and beanstalks to climb.

Knots to untangle

and boats to be sailed,

hills to be rolled down

and peaks to be scaled.

and letters to write . . .

stars to sleep under,

friends to hold tight.

Lives to imagine

and hands to be held,

poems to whisper

and songs to
be yelled.

Lessons to learn
and books to be read ...

each holding a glimpse
of what lies ahead.

On land and by air,
and in dreams that come true,

with blue skies and sunshine,

this world awaits YOU.